SERVICE DOGS

by Dale Jones

Consultant: Karen Shirk, CEO, 4 Paws for Ability

Minneapolis, Minnesota

Photo credits: Cover and 1, ©Huntstock/Getty Images; 2, ©Matt Benoit/Shutterstock; 3, ©Eric Isselee/Shutterstock; 4, ©Africa Studio/Shutterstock; 5, ©Maki Nakamura/Getty Images; 6, ©Sergio Azenha/Alamy; 7, ©Arterra Picture Library/Alamy; 8, ©William Mullins/Alamy; 9, ©Pat Canova/Alamy; 10, ©The Washington Post /Getty Images; 11, ©Huntstock/Getty Images; 12, ©Zipster969/Wikimedia; 13, ©adamkaz/Getty Images; 14, ©Mark Hunt/Newscom; 15, ©Boston Globe/Getty Images; 16, ©Halfpoint/Shutterstock; 17, ©Wang He/Stringer/Getty Images; 18, ©Karen Patterson/Alamy; 19, ©ZUMA Press Inc/Alamy; 20, ©Alistair Heap/Alamy; 21, ©MintImages/Shutterstock; 22, ©MediaNews Group/Orange County Register via Getty Images/Getty Images; 23, ©Sergio Azenha/Alamy

President: Jen Jenson
Director of Product Development: Spencer Brinker
Senior Editor: Allison Juda
Associate Editor: Charly Haley
Designer: Colin O'Dea

Library of Congress Cataloging-in-Publication Data

Names: Jones, Dale, 1990- author.
Title: Service dogs / Dale Jones ; consultant, Karen Shirk, CEO, 4 Paws for Ability.
Description: Minneapolis, Minnesota : Bearport Publishing Company, [2022] | Series: Heroic dogs | Includes bibliographical references and index.
Identifiers: LCCN 2021009303 (print) | LCCN 2021009304 (ebook) | ISBN 9781636911199 (library binding) | ISBN 9781636911281 (paperback) | ISBN 9781636911373 (ebook)
Subjects: LCSH: Service dogs--Juvenile literature.
Classification: LCC HV1569.6 .J66 2022 (print) | LCC HV1569.6 (ebook) | DDC 362.4/0483--dc23
LC record available at https://lccn.loc.gov/2021009303
LC ebook record available at https://lccn.loc.gov/2021009304

Copyright ©2022 Bearport Publishing Company. All rights reserved. No part of this publication may be reproduced in whole or in part, stored in any retrieval system, or transmitted in any form or by any means, electronic, mechanical, photocopying, recording, or otherwise, without written permission from the publisher.

For more information, write to Bearport Publishing, 5357 Penn Avenue South, Minneapolis, MN 55419.

Contents

A Furry Helper 4

Lending a Paw 6

Learning the Basics 8

At Your Service 10

Mobility Dogs 12

Another Pair of Ears 14

Guiding Eyes 16

Calming Canines 18

A Nose for Safety 20

Meet a Real Service Dog 22

Glossary 23

Index 24

Read More 24

Learn More Online 24

About the Author 24

A Furry Helper

Smoke rises from a hot oven, and an alarm starts beeping. But the person in the next room is deaf and can't hear the alarm. How will she know there is danger?

Her service dog springs into action! The dog touches its owner with its wet nose. Then, the dog leads her into the kitchen so she can turn off the oven. When it's safe, the owner thanks her furry helper.

Service dogs can help people of any age—even kids!

A service dog stays near its owner and is always ready to help.

Lending a Paw

Service dogs are working dogs that help people in different ways. Some service dogs hear for people who can't. Others help people with **disabilities** who may have a hard time getting from place to place. Some service dogs even bring objects to people who can't pick things up for themselves. These **canines** can be trained to help their owners with all sorts of tasks.

Sometimes, a service dog will wear a vest. Never pet a working dog—it has an important job to do!

Service dogs often help with everyday tasks, including shopping for groceries.

Learning the Basics

Service dogs begin the hard work of training from an early age. When they're puppies, they live with foster families who teach the pups basic **cues** such as sit and stay. The puppies also learn to be calm and quiet in public.

Puppies in training live with their foster families until they are about a year or a year and a half old.

An important part of early service dog training is for the dogs to learn to be on their best behavior at all times.

At Your Service

With the basics behind them, the dogs can move on to learning how to help people. They often go through this part of training at special schools. Dogs learn different skills for different kinds of service. Some dogs are taught to push buttons or fetch items. Other dogs may learn to **alert** their **handlers** when there is a change in the person's health.

They say hands are for helping, but mouths can be useful, too! Service dogs can be trained to carry things in their mouths.

Service dogs may learn to push buttons to open doors or call elevators.

Mobility Dogs

Sometimes, a service dog helps a person who can't move on their own! Mobility dogs are trained to help people who use wheelchairs, walkers, scooters, or canes. If a handler has trouble reaching objects or carrying them, a mobility dog can help. These service dogs can pick up dropped objects or carry things. Some even open and close drawers or turn lights on and off.

Some people have trouble walking or standing. A service dog can be trained to help keep a person going.

Service dogs go everywhere with their handlers.

13

Another Pair of Ears

Service dogs that help people who are deaf or hard of hearing are called hearing dogs. These helpers are trained to listen for sounds and alert their handlers. Hearing dogs will let their handlers know if there is a knock at the door, if an alarm sounds, or if the phone rings.

Some people don't speak. They may use hand **signals** to give their hearing dogs cues.

A hearing dog may alert its handler when the handler's name is called.

Hearing dogs know they can't get their handlers' attention by barking. Instead, these service dogs alert by touching handlers with their paws or noses.

Guiding Eyes

For people who are blind or have trouble seeing, guide dogs are the perfect fit. These service dogs help their handlers **navigate** the world around them. If a handler needs to go outside, the team heads out together. The handler gives cues to tell the dog where to go and when to stop. The dog's guiding eyes help keep its owner safe.

A guide dog makes sure its handler doesn't hit their head on things up high, trip over things on the ground, or get hurt while crossing the street.

A guide dog usually walks on the left side of its handler.

Calming Canines

Some service dogs are trained to help people who have **mental disorders** such as panic attacks or other sudden feelings of stress. Mental disorders may make it difficult for people to do everyday things. A service dog can help its handler calm down or bring them a phone to call for help. These comforting **companions** help people feel safe.

A service dog may help its handler feel calmer by leaning into their body.

Mental disorders usually cannot be seen from the outside. That can make it especially important for these service dogs to be able to do their work.

A Nose for Safety

Another kind of service dog helps people who have dangerous **allergies** to foods or other things. Allergy alert dogs use their powerful noses to smell for the things that could make their handlers sick. They alert if they find anything. Then, the person knows to be careful.

Scientists think that about one-third of a dog's brain is used for smell. Allergy alert dogs put this strong sense to good use!

A service dog will often stay with the same handler its whole working life.

Although some people have challenges getting through life, they're not alone. Service dogs are four-legged heroes that are ready to help!

Meet a Real Service Dog

Professor John Terhorst worked with 16 other dogs before he met Yan in 2015, and the pair has been together ever since then. The service dog helps the professor get around in his wheelchair.

Yan helps John as he teaches his chemistry classes. The dog carries John's tablet and opens doors so John can wheel through them. Everyone smiles when they see the service dog at work!

Yan knows more than 40 different cues to help John with daily life.

Glossary

alert to bring something to a person's attention

allergies medical conditions that cause someone to become sick after eating, touching, or breathing something that is harmless to most people, such as peanuts

canines dogs

companions animals or people who spend time with others

cues words or actions that signal a dog to do something

disabilities conditions that make it hard for a person to do everyday things, such as walking, seeing, or hearing

handlers people who are helped by service dogs

mental disorders illnesses that affect the mind

navigate to find one's way from place to place

signals gestures or movements that mean something specific

Index

alert 10, 14–15, 20
allergy alert dogs 20
cues 8, 14, 16, 22
disabilities 6
foster families 8
guide dogs 16–17

hearing dogs 14–15
mobility dogs 12
signals 14
training 6, 8–10, 12, 14, 18
vests 6

Read More

Jones, Dale. *Guide Dogs (Heroic Dogs)*. Minneapolis: Bearport Publishing, 2022.

Murray, Julie. *Service Animals (Working Animals)*. Minneapolis: Abdo Zoom, 2020.

Learn More Online

1. Go to **www.factsurfer.com**
2. Enter "**Service Dogs**" into the search box.
3. Click on the cover of this book to see a list of websites.

About the Author

Dale Jones lives in Los Angeles, California, with his family and two dogs.

24